UPDATE:

Date Rape

by Alexandra Bandon

Crestwood House
New York
Maxwell Macmillan Canada
Toronto
Maxwell Macmillan International
New York   Oxford   Singapore   Sydney

Cartoon drawings by Jim Kirschman

PHOTO CREDITS

Cover: Brian Vaughan
Bettye Lane: 9,42
AP Wide World Photos: 12
Brian Vaughan: 16, 28, 33, 37
John Forasté/Brown University: 23

Crestwood House
Macmillan Publishing Company
866 Third Avenue
New York, NY 10022

Maxwell Macmillan Canada, Inc.
1200 Eglinton Avenue East
Suite 200
Don Mills, Ontario M3C 3N1

Macmillan Publishing Company is a part of the Maxwell Communication Group of Companies

First edition
Printed in the United States of America

10 9 8 7 6 5 4 3 2 1

Library of Congress Cataloging-in-Publication Data

Bandon, Alexandra.
    Date rape / by Alexandra Bandon — 1st ed.
        p.   cm. — (Update)
        Summary: Discusses the phenomenon known as acquaintance, or date, rape, describing situations in which it occurs, how to avoid this crime, and where to get help if you have been a victim.
        Includes index.
        ISBN 0-89686-806-0   ISBN 0-382-24755-8 (pbk)
        1. Acquaintance rape—United States—Juvenile literature. 2. Rape—United States—Prevention—Juvenile literature. 3. Rape victims—Services for—United States—Juvenile literature. [1. Acquaintance rape. 2. Rape. 3. Dating violence.] I. Title. II. Series: Update.
    HV6561.B33   1994
    362.88'3—dc20   93-24063

Contents

WHAT IS DATE RAPE?

When you mention the word **rape**, most people think of a crazed stranger jumping out from a dark corner and attacking a helpless woman. But most rapes actually happen between two people who already know each other. The victim and the attacker may be good friends, boyfriend and girlfriend, or even husband and wife.

A Definition
In every state, by law, rape is forced sexual intercourse, or sexual intercourse without the **consent** of both people.

In many states, rape laws include other forced sexual acts as well as intercourse. Some states also have removed language in their laws that point specifically to men as attackers and women as victims. That's because a man can be a victim of rape as well. And some states have taken the word *rape* out of the laws and replaced it with the term **sexual assault**.

A rapist does not always use a weapon. Sometimes an attacker uses physical force, or just the threat of force,

---

Did You Know...?

• **About 4 out of 5 rape victims (around 80 percent) knew their attacker.**

• **Most victims of date rape are not on the first date with their attackers. They are usually on their fourth or fifth date.**

• **A majority of rapes occur in the home of either the victim or the attacker.**

"I asked him to stop. . ."

Kathy met Rick at a party one night in college. She had noticed him because he had intense blue eyes. "I would catch him looking at me," she says. "I thought it was really cool. Sometimes I'd even stare back."

Kathy remembers that Rick was really sweet and charming, telling her that she had a beautiful smile. As the party ended, Kathy agreed to let Rick walk her home.

Back at her apartment, Kathy invited Rick inside to talk. To avoid waking her roommates, Kathy suggested they go into her bedroom.

After a while, they started kissing on her bed. Rick put his hand under her shirt, and she didn't push it away. When he reached for her belt buckle, however, she resisted.

Kathy still has a look of surprise on her face when she remembers what happened next. "Suddenly he was on top of me, pinning me down with his legs while his hands were pulling my pants down. I asked him to stop, but he wouldn't listen. I could hardly breathe because he had his full weight on top of me."

When Kathy started to cry, Rick got mad. "He just looked at me and said, 'Why are you crying?' Then he slapped me really hard and growled, 'Don't cry.' I was so scared, I just lay there."

Rick forced sex on Kathy. Then he fell asleep in her apartment. She couldn't sleep all night. When Rick left the next morning, he told her he'd call her later.

"I couldn't believe he said that," says Kathy. "All I could think was what a jerk he was. At the time, I didn't realize that Rick had raped me. I mean, I had let him in. I had kissed him and let him touch me. I just thought I had done something wrong."

instead of a knife or a gun. In other cases an attacker might rape a victim who is physically or mentally unable to consent to sex. For instance, a victim may have had too much to drink or may have taken drugs.

Date rape occurs when the victim and the attacker know each other and are on a date by choice. It could be their first or their fiftieth date. The couple could be just friends or dating steadily.

Date rape is part of the broader category of **acquaintance rape**, which is rape by a person the victim knows but isn't dating. The attacker could be a neighbor, a doctor, a minister, a classmate, a teacher, a relative, or anyone else the victim knows. Many people use the term *date rape* to describe all forms of acquaintance rape. Another kind of acquaintance rape is **marital rape**, which is rape between husband and wife.

Is It Really Rape?
Some people believe that date rape is not as serious as **stranger rape**. They argue that a woman isn't really raped unless she is brutally attacked by an armed person who takes her by surprise. To them, date rape couldn't be as harmful to the victim because she knows her attacker.

In reality, however, date rape is just as harmful—and often more harmful—to the victim. Not only does she experience physical and sexual assault, but she is attacked by someone she trusts, maybe even loves. Now she's no longer sure of whom to trust. Often the victim feels confused about why this has happened to her. She may even blame herself for what happened.

Most of the rapes we hear about on the news or in the papers are stranger rapes. A victim of date rape may not recognize her experience as a crime. But probably she will suffer the same reactions and experience the same problems that most victims of rape go through.

Both stranger rape and date rape happen because the attacker is trying to control the victim. But there is one main difference between the two. Stranger rape begins with a man's plan to force himself on the woman. The attacker rapes his victim to **degrade** and hurt her.

But date rape begins as planned sex. The attacker begins to think that he and his partner are going to have sex. When his partner doesn't respond, he forces himself on her. He believes he deserves to have sex with her or that the woman is obliged to consent to his advances.

Some people believe that date rape shouldn't be called rape. Although the woman said no, these people think, she really meant yes. They say that the woman feels guilty afterward and wants to save her reputation—that's why she accuses the man of rape. The two people were kissing or fondling each other, and therefore both partners intended to have sex.

Others say that the way men and women play at sex often includes forced intercourse—that violence in sex can be normal. According to this view, women are supposed to say no and resist, and men are supposed to force them.

Many men who have raped a date don't even realize that what they did was rape and that the act was illegal. Because they believe that most women want to be "convinced" that they should have sex, the men might think that their behavior was perfectly normal. To them, they "scored." Many victims say their attackers even asked them out again, acting as if nothing unusual occurred.

Our culture supports the notion that men are supposed to be strong and use **aggression**. Movies show men grabbing women for a "romantic" clinch. How many movies and TV

Some American universities sponsor "Take Back the Night" rallies, in which women peacefully protest against sexual assault crimes.

shows have you seen in which the man grabs the woman and kisses her against her will, only to have her become putty in his arms? The films *Gone with the Wind* and *Basic Instinct* are two examples. In music, songs often describe how a woman "made" the man do something, or how he "couldn't help himself."

Many misunderstandings exist about attackers and victims in sexual assaults. Yet one thing alone decides whether rape occurred, and that is whether or not both people consented to have sex.

Four Famous Examples The headlines said it all: "MIKE TYSON SENTENCED TO 6 YEARS FOR RAPE."

In 1992 the legendary heavyweight boxing champion was found guilty of raping a Miss Black America Pageant contestant. Tyson had invited the woman to some parties in Indianapolis, Indiana, where the pageant was taking place. Instead he took her to his hotel room, where he sexually assaulted her.

Tyson's lawyer tried to show that the woman knew she would be having sex with Tyson when she agreed to go out with him. But the jury believed that she thought they would be going sightseeing. In fact, the woman had invited a friend to come along. She'd even brought a camera with her.

A few months earlier, William Kennedy Smith, a nephew of Senator Edward Kennedy and of former President John Kennedy, had been found not guilty of rape. He was

When three young men from Glen Ridge, New Jersey, were found guilty of sexual assault, some people thought justice had been done. The jury had ruled that the former high school football players had sexually assaulted a retarded schoolmate with a bat, a stick, and a broomstick. Many people thought the young men would pay for their crimes.

But the three men were given a light sentence of up to 15 years in a youth facility. They will probably serve no more than 22 months. And the defendants were free on bail until their appeals were decided, which may take many years.

In fact, the sentence in this case is not far off from the national average. According to a Justice Department survey taken in 1989, the average time served by a convicted rapist was only 29 months.

Still, rape victim advocates were appalled by the meager punishment. They believed it sent a clear message to rape victims: Society obviously doesn't consider rape such a serious offense, since rapists can get off so easily. The legal system doesn't offer victims much protection.

accused of forcing sex on a woman he had met in a bar during Easter weekend of 1991. But the prosecutor in the Palm Beach, Florida, case failed to prove that Smith and his accuser had sex without her consent.

Smith testified that they had sex twice with her consent. Then, he said, she became angry when he called her by the wrong name.

In deciding the case, the jury kept in mind that the woman had left the bar with Smith and had removed her pantyhose,

Mike Tyson (center), the former heavyweight boxing champion, was convicted of date rape in 1992.

found later in her car. The judge refused to allow as evidence three sworn statements from other women who said Smith had raped each of them on earlier occasions.

The Tyson and Smith cases made headlines because they involved famous people. But two other cases made the papers recently because of the circumstances surrounding the rapes.

In 1991, six students at St. John's University in New York were charged with raping a fellow student. She had accepted a ride home with one man. When they stopped off at his house, he gave her several vodka drinks.

Three of the men were found not guilty. The other three pleaded guilty to lesser charges. The man who had driven the victim home and offered her the drinks admitted that he had gotten the woman drunk in order to take advantage of her.

In 1992–1993, four teens in New Jersey were tried for sexually assaulting a mildly retarded girl. With an IQ of 64, the girl was not believed to have the mental ability to consent to sexual acts. The lawyers for the four accused teens tried to show that the girl wanted to have sex with the boys. Three of the boys were found guilty of charges relating to sexually assaulting a mentally handicapped person.

These four news-making cases show how people misunderstand consent. Each case is an example of the different ways people can perceive sex and date rape.

THE VICTIM

Look around you. Think of all the people you know. You probably know someone who has been date-raped.

Studies show that, among women in general, 1 out of every 5 has been raped by someone she knew. And most date rapes happen to women between the ages of 15 and 24.

But rape is the most underreported of all violent crimes. Only 1 out of every 100 acquaintance rapes is reported to the police.

Unreported Rape

One reason rape goes unreported is that the victim is afraid she'll be blamed. A woman who is raped is often questioned about what she was wearing or what she did to provoke an attack.

Sometimes the victim might think she won't be believed, even by friends and family. She might be afraid that they'll blame her for "causing trouble."

Some people may feel that the victim doesn't look upset enough. But many victims seem calm because they are almost numb from shock.

Other people will not believe a date rape victim because

Did You Know...?

• Acquaintance rape is most likely to happen to women between the ages of 15 and 24.

• Until 1979, in most states it was not a crime for a husband to rape his wife.

• About 10 percent of rape victims are men. More than 50 percent of male rape victims knew their attacker.

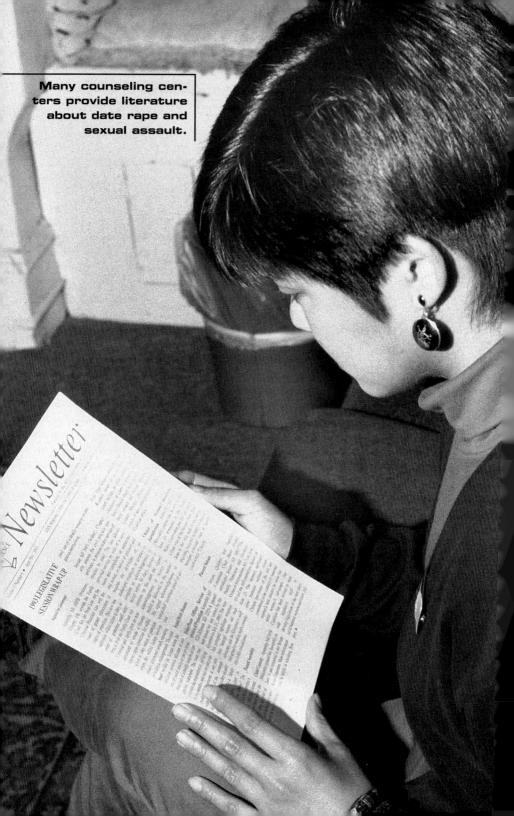

Many counseling centers provide literature about date rape and sexual assault.

she does not have bruises and because there is no witness. But many other crimes have no witness. A mugging might take just a few seconds, and the victim may not see the face of her mugger. Yet people usually believe a woman who says she was mugged. A rape victim might be attacked for hours, face-to-face with her attacker. Yet people do not always believe she was raped.

Another reason a date rape victim may not report the crime is that she blames herself. She wonders whether she might have prevented the rape by acting differently.

Sometimes victims don't report a rape because they don't realize they have been raped. It may take days, months, or even years before a victim will admit that she was attacked. Some women may never realize it.

Many victims think their attack was not rape because they knew their attacker. The word *rape* brings up such ugly and violent images that victims may be unable to admit that someone they trusted would commit such an act.

The Victim's Personality
Victims of date rape have few characteristics in common. Many people believe that "easy" women are more likely to be raped. But studies show that all kinds of women can become victims. There is no one type.

However, victims often lack self-confidence. Most rapes occur when the victim is feeling unsure about herself. Such a woman is more likely to ignore warning signs about a potential attacker because she wants to be accepted. Many date rapes happen during a victim's first year of college or first year in a new school, when she is trying to make new friends.

Sometimes a woman can be raped again by the same attacker. This is called **revictimization**. It is not uncommon, mostly because some victims don't admit to themselves what happened.

When a woman keeps dating the man who raped her, she often does it to fool herself into believing that what happened was normal. Unfortunately, she will probably be raped again before the relationship ends.

Men as Victims
The majority of rapes involve men attacking women. But men are sometimes victims, too. In fact, about one tenth of acquaintance rape victims are men attacked by other men. Men who are raped have an even harder time telling anyone about their attacks. They think they will be made fun of for allowing themselves to be overpowered.

When a man is attacked by another man, the incident may not have anything to do with whether the attacker or the victim is **heterosexual** or **homosexual**. But many victims think they will be labeled as gay and shunned if they tell anyone. They may also worry that the attack means that they are gay.

If the victim *is* a homosexual and was on a date with his attacker, then he may not tell anyone because he doesn't want the police or his family to find out he's gay.

When a Man Is Raped. . .

Duane had never imagined that a heterosexual man could be raped. "I figured when a guy raped another guy, it was something between gay men," says Duane. When it happened to him, he had difficulty understanding why the rape had occurred.

During his sophomore year of college, Duane befriended Sam. They enjoyed many of the same interests, and Duane looked up to Sam, a popular guy on campus.

One night at a party, they got into an argument. "I can't remember what we were fighting about. Sam just kept calling me names and putting me down."

Both Sam and Duane had been drinking, which fueled the argument. "I got annoyed with Sam. I decided to go crash in my room. I barely got undressed, I think, before I passed out," recalls Duane.

"I woke up, I don't know how much later, to find Sam on top of me. He was raping me. I tried to struggle, but he weighed much more than me. He was pushing my face into the pillow. I had no strength and I was almost suffocating."

The next day, Duane had a swollen black eye. "I had to tell everyone that I had left the party and gotten into a brawl with some guy.

"I started keeping to myself," Duane recalls. "And I avoided Sam." The resident adviser in Duane's dorm sensed the problem. "She asked me if Sam was the guy I'd gotten into a fight with. I figured I could at least tell her that much, since everyone had seen me and Sam arguing that night.

"Then she asked me if that was all that had happened." She suspected that Duane might have been sexually assaulted. "I was so relieved to finally tell someone."

The resident adviser took the case anonymously to the school's psychologist. The doctor recommended separate counseling for both Duane and Sam.

"I kept thinking that Sam was gay," says Duane. "I was afraid he thought that I was gay, too. And I figured anyone I told would think the same. I didn't realize then that Sam was not gay at all. Homosexuality had nothing to do with what he did to me. He was only trying to overpower me."

ONLY 22% OF ALL RAPE VICTIMS ARE ASSAULTED BY STRANGERS.

There is no such thing as the typical date rapist. Most rapists are men. But there is no standard physical appearance for a rapist. Each attacker is different, and each attacks differently. However, there are some things that most date rapists have in common.

The "Typical" Rapist
Half the men arrested for rape are under 24 years old. The average age of a rapist is 18½.

Date rapists are usually very sociable men who get along with people. That's why they are able to be in situations that may lead to date rape. If they weren't pleasant or appealing in some way, they would never gain their victims' trust enough to be alone with them.

A date rapist doesn't plan to rape his victim. Unlike a stranger rapist, who plans to rape, a date rapist plans to have sex. He mistakes his date's interest in going out for an interest in having sex. Then when his date refuses or resists, he rapes her.

A man who commits date rape is likely to repeat his crime. Many rapists continue to rape until they are caught

Did You Know...?

• One study of teenage rape victims found that 97 percent were attacked by a boyfriend, date, or friend.

• Unlike stranger rapists, date rapists do not have problems being outspoken among other people.

and punished. Some date rapists commit the crime even after they've been reported to the police.

Danger Signs Young women concerned about date rape should watch for danger signs in the personality of men they are dating.

Beware of someone who makes decisions for you without asking. That includes telling you what to wear or how to act, insisting on paying for everything on the date, and telling you who you can and cannot be friends with. This person must control all situations. He'll probably get angry when you try to do things your way or if you offer to pay for dinner or a movie during your date.

Avoid guys who don't listen to you or pretend not to hear you. Chances are, they won't listen later when you tell them that you don't want to have intercourse.

A potential attacker might show anger toward people who are weaker than he is, especially women. He might be unkind to children or pets. He might put down women in general. He might even become violent at times, pushing or grabbing other people to get his way.

Women should watch the way a man approaches them. Does he get too close? Does he invade your personal space, even when you ask him not to? Does he touch you when you tell him not to? Does he get angry when something you do frustrates him? Does he talk down to you or insult you? Does he try to make you look or feel stupid? Does he get jealous for no reason?

Brown University students perform a theater piece called <u>When a Kiss Is Not Just a Kiss</u> as part of a sexual assault peer education program.

Be particularly careful of someone who urges you to drink alcohol against your will or to take drugs, especially if he gets angry if you refuse. He may be trying to weaken your resolve so you'll have sex with him. And remember that your physical strength decreases if you're drunk or high on drugs.

Be on guard if your date drinks heavily or uses drugs. Most attackers are drunk or high when they commit rape.

The most important thing to remember is to trust your instincts about people. If someone makes you uneasy, stay away.

Avoiding **RAPE**

To say that one can prevent rape is misleading. But a woman can keep many things in mind when approaching a date. Women can try to avoid situations that might end in rape.

Avoiding Rape Situations (Women)

Women need to remember to communicate. Tell your date firmly and loudly *no* when he does something you don't like. Your date can't know what it is that you want or don't want unless you tell him.

Don't use the word *no* as a ploy to get a man to flatter you more until he convinces you. He may end up not believing *no* when you really mean it.

You have the right to refuse anything you don't want to do. But remember to say it right away. Just because you agreed to kiss or be fondled does not mean you agreed to intercourse. Your date has no right to demand it. It's okay to want some things and not others, but don't be inconsistent with your **body language**. Don't worry about embar-

---

Did You Know...?

• Acquaintance rape is most likely to occur when a man has paid for the whole date, when the attacker is drunk, or when the couple is alone.

• About 50 percent of high school students surveyed say that forced sex is okay if the man spent a lot of money or the woman excited him.

---

rassing yourself or your date or about appearing uptight.

Don't make it easier for him to attack by going to an isolated spot. Agree to meet in a public place on your first date. And always have enough money with you to get yourself home if you need to. Many victims say they were forced to choose between giving in to an attacker or being left stranded in a dangerous or deserted location.

Talk about where you want to go and what you want to do so your date knows that he doesn't have all the control. Offer to pay for some of the date so he won't feel that you "owe" him something in return for spending money on you.

Avoid or limit alcohol consumption and stay away from drugs. Drugs and alcohol can affect a person's judgment and are often a partial cause of rapes. A man who is drunk or high may think he's seducing a woman when he's really raping her. He may feed a woman drinks or drugs to get her defenses down. A victim who is drunk or high might misjudge the person she is with. And some victims have been attacked after they've passed out.

Most of all, follow your instincts. If someone makes you uncomfortable, then leave. If you think someone might be dangerous, trust your judgment and avoid being with that person. Don't assume that your date's behavior will change when the two of you are alone.

Avoiding Rape Situations (Men)

Men can avoid committing date rape by understanding that rape

A Bad Situation

Yolanda met Jerome, a star football player, at a party after one of the games. "He was tall, with a great body," she recalls, "and everybody thought he was so funny. He kept paying me all this attention and I just loved it."

At the end of the party, Yolanda agreed to let Jerome drive her home. She didn't realize that he'd done some cocaine. When he suggested they stop off somewhere to talk, she agreed.

"He took me to this place where the kids go to park sometimes—this deserted airstrip," Yolanda recalls. "We were in the backseat making out. And he put his hand on my chest, over my dress. I kind of moved it away. But then he put his hand on my leg and tried to move it up my dress. I was wearing a really short dress, so he didn't have far to go, you know?"

Yolanda moved his hand away again. Then Jerome asked her why she didn't want him to "make her feel good."

"I said, 'Because it's my body!' and left it at that. We started kissing again, and there's his hand again on my leg. I tried to move it away, but this time it wouldn't budge. Sometimes a guy sort of fights you and you have to really push to get him to stop. But usually he gives in. But Jerome's hand was like a rock."

Yolanda didn't know what to do. "I really started to panic," she recalls. "All I could think was, here's this guy, 6 foot 4, over 200 pounds. There's no way I'm stronger than him. All these bad scenes started racing through my head and I got really scared. I just yelled out, 'Stop it!' as loud as I could. That's when he took his hand away, and I sat up and moved to the other side of the car."

After that night, Yolanda decided to stay away from isolated places with her dates. "I learned my lesson. I don't go off anymore with a guy I don't know. And I'm real loud now when I tell them to back off."

Support groups can help rape survivors deal with confusion, anger, and grief.

affects them as well. Imagine how you would feel if your mother, girlfriend, or sister were raped.

The first rule to remember is that *no* means *no*. *No* does not mean *yes*, *maybe*, or *convince me*. Don't try to force a woman to have sex when she says she doesn't want to. That might be construed as **coercion**. Don't push her with physical force. And don't try to talk her into it. When a woman says no, stop. If you are unsure whether or not she said no, ask her. If you are still unsure, then stop anyway.

Remember that no woman "deserves" to be raped or mistreated by a man. The way a woman dresses or acts has nothing to do with whether she means to have sex.

Become aware of the sexual attitudes of people around you. You may be surprised at what you hear. Some men believe the myth that having sex with a woman, even if it's forced, is a victory. The number of women you sleep with doesn't say anything about your manhood.

Talk about date rape with your friends. Let them know when you think they're not treating a woman with respect or if they're being abusive. Tell them you won't tolerate or participate in that kind of behavior.

Stop friends who may be about to abuse a woman or force her into sex. Never join in group sex with one woman, especially if she's drunk or high. (Several men forcing sex on a woman is called **gang rape**.)

Most important, listen to your date and make sure you know what she does and doesn't want. Don't be afraid to ask her if something you want to do is okay with her, and make sure you ask without putting pressure on her. If she says it's not okay, then respect her and *stop*.

WHEN RAPE HAPPENS

Despite growing awareness of date rape, some women find themselves trapped in rape situations. Counselors have talked to women who avoided possible rapes, and have learned what they did to escape attacks.

Under Attack
Women who stayed calm were able to think clearly and protect themselves. First they decided how much danger they were in—whether or not they could scream or run for help, or whether the attacker had a weapon. Quick action always gave the woman an advantage, since the attacker wasn't giving her much time.

Some women were able to stall the attacker by talking to him. They tried to distract him with normal conversation. Sometimes this distraction gave the women a chance to run away.

Many attackers were caught off guard when victims

Did You Know...?

• Many rape victims don't seek help until several years after the attack.

• In 1989 a Florida jury of three men and three women found a man not guilty of kidnapping a 22-year-old woman and repeatedly raping her at knife-point. One juror said, "We felt she asked for it because of the way she was dressed." The victim was wearing a lace miniskirt and no underwear.

screamed and yelled. Their cries also alerted people nearby that an attack was going on. But in some cases the screaming made the attacker more angry. Some women who were trapped in a car with their attackers used the horn to attract attention.

Some women used words or behavior that turned the attacker off to the whole idea of a "romantic evening." They told the attacker they had their period or a **sexually transmitted disease**. Some women claimed to be pregnant. Other women did something unattractive, like picking their noses or pretending to be crazy.

Some victims hurt the attacker to get away. Chances are the women wouldn't have won if they had tried to wrestle the man, so they poked him in the eyes or kneed him in the crotch, then fled.

But each woman had to be very definite when she tried to defend herself with physical force. Those who didn't succeed only made the attacker more angry. Self-defense courses or books on the subject can be very helpful for women who want to learn more about fighting back.

Some victims were forced to give in to rape. Yielding to an attacker is not the wrong choice. It doesn't mean the victim gave her consent, either. She simply looked at her situation and felt that her only choice was to submit, rather than risk greater physical harm or even death.

After the Attack
What's the most helpful thing a

victim can do immediately after a rape? She should not blame herself.

Then she should tell someone she trusts what happened. Friends are often supportive. Some parents are understanding because they are concerned for their child's safety. Some parents, however, don't believe their daughter's version of the story and are not very supportive. Rape crisis hot lines (in the phone book under "Rape") have counselors who are trained to help victims through the recovery process. Everything the victim tells them is confidential.

Rape victims should get medical attention within 72 hours

A doctor explains the different parts of a rape evidence kit to a sexual assault survivor.

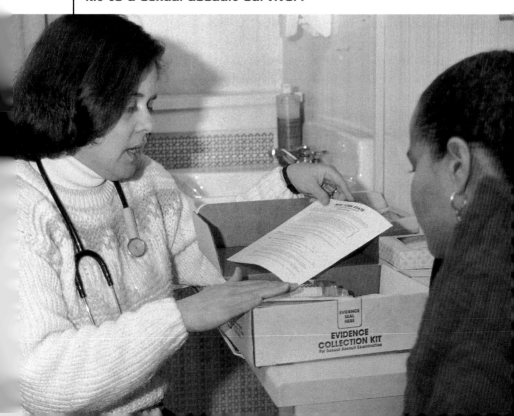

Painful Memories

Bianca was raped in her first year of college by her boyfriend, Adam. Seven years later, Bianca's voice still shakes as she talks about the lingering effects of the attack.

"Every fall, around September, I find myself getting very depressed." Bianca was attacked in September.

"That incident still has a big effect on the way I deal with other people. What has it been, seven years? But I still have a lot of trouble getting physically close to anyone. I don't like being touched, by men or women, when I'm not expecting it. I have a tendency to stiffen up. Even my brother has commented on it. Imagine how bad it is with a guy who's trying to get romantic!

"Specific things about Adam still bother me, too. If I smell the cologne he used to wear, I can't even talk to the person wearing it or be nearby, because it brings back such vivid memories of Adam."

Bit by bit, Bianca is working through her feelings. "Lately, at least I've begun to come to terms with not being ashamed about what happened. It wasn't my fault, what Adam did to me. In my senior year of college, I lectured to freshmen about the date rape problem on campus. And in the last year or two when I begin to get deeply involved in a relationship, I explain what happened to me. It makes me more comfortable with a new physical relationship.

"That doesn't mean Adam doesn't still get to me," Bianca admits. "Recently, someone mentioned him to me without warning. I was so shook up, I couldn't say anything. Then I was distracted for the rest of the day. Some parts of it will never go away, I guess."

(three days) after the attack. The victim should not wash, shower, change her clothes, or brush her teeth before she is examined. If she does, valuable evidence can be lost.

If she goes to the local emergency room and explains that she has been raped, the hospital will use an **evidence collection kit**. The staff will take samples of hairs, clothing fibers, blood, saliva, or **semen** left on the victim by the attacker. However, not all hospital staffs are trained to help rape victims. The examination process can be awkward and embarrassing.

The hospital will treat the victim's injuries. It will also test for sexually transmitted diseases and pregnancy. These tests can still be done even if the victim didn't go to a hospital within the first three days. Some doctors may ask the victim to talk to someone about being tested later for **HIV,** the virus that causes AIDS.

Reporting the Rape to the Police
Rape victims can report the attack to the police, who may take the evidence from the hospital. Reporting makes some victims feel safer. Women who press charges by publicly accusing their attacker are asked for details about what happened, and will have to describe the incident several times to a number of people.

Victims then tell their stories in court for cases handled by a **district attorney,** or prosecutor who works for the city or state, not the victim. An attacker who is found guilty can be given a **sentence** of jail or **probation**, or be sent to counseling. The job of the lawyer for the **defendant** (the attacker) is to keep the prosecutor from proving rape. Usually the lawyer does this by trying to show that the victim is lying.

Victims who don't press charges can still file an anonymous report with the police. In most states that report stays on file in case the attacker is arrested for another crime. If the police or the prosecutor comes across such a report, he or she will be more likely to make sure the next case goes to court.

Women who have been raped should get counseling, even if it's a long time after the rape happened. Rape hot line counselors can help right after the attack. Later they can recommend support groups that meet regularly. Participants share experiences and talk about their feelings.

Victims also might need time away from work or school. Some women need to sort through their feelings before they go back to normal life.

Recovering

Recovering from rape is a long, hard process. Stranger rape and acquaintance rape victims both go through the recovery process.

A victim of rape doesn't just get over it and forget it. Instead, she may experience many different moods and reactions to her attack. None of those reactions is wrong. Each rape victim has a unique healing process.

Some victims appear calm after the attack. Others sob hysterically. Every victim needs to sort out feelings about himself or herself, the attacker, and the incident.

A counselor can help a rape survivor get on the road to recovery.

Though each victim's reaction to rape is different, most victims experience at least one of a group of feelings about their attack. A victim may feel angry, ashamed, depressed, guilty, or scared. She may even want to kill herself. She might wrongly blame herself for the attack. She may appear nervous or jumpy. Some victims have trouble eating and sleeping. Some women feel as if they will never be clean again.

One of the first things rape victims want to do is to take a shower. The victim will try to scrub the smell of the attacker off her body, sometimes with more than one shower. She may also have physical reactions, like severe headaches, that come from being upset. She may feel sick or even vomit.

But the aftermath of rape lingers. Rape victims experience many psychological effects. These effects can be serious or minor, depending on the personality of the victim.

A victim of an acquaintance rape is likely to be anxious. She is usually in shock because she was surprised by her attacker's behavior. One minute she believed she could trust this person. The next minute that same person was attacking her.

Victims may also feel confused and angry. Some victims of date rape don't understand what happened to them. They just know that they had a bad experience.

Often a victim blames herself for the attack. She may question herself and her behavior before, during, and after the rape. Did I say or do something to give him the impression I wanted to sleep with him? Did I fight back enough? Should I have let him into the house?

When some of these bad feelings become too much for a victim, she may become depressed, shutting herself off from the world. Severely depressed women might even think about killing themselves. It is not unusual for a rape victim to consider suicide.

Rape can also affect the way the victim deals with other people. She may avoid contact with people. She may begin to distrust others, especially men. Many victims have trou-

Circle of Women

At one rape support group in New York City, seven women sit in a circle and talk about their experiences and recoveries. Each one of them is different. Some are white, some are African American, some are Hispanic. Some are old and some are young. But all the women have one thing in common. They were raped by people they knew.

Helene didn't come to the group until 15 years after her attack—about a year ago.

Maddie just joined today. Her attack happened two weeks ago.

Gina, who was raped by her stepfather as a child, came for help after her boyfriend did the same thing. "I love the women here," says Gina. "It's the only time I can talk about my attacks and not have people look at me with that 'so that's why your life's so messed up' look."

Patty agrees. She was raped by a man she met in a bar one night. "It kills me when I see trials on TV and they ask the victim why she did this or why she did that. Like she's supposed to be responsible for what the guy's doing!"

Maddie looks scared. She hasn't talked yet. Finally she says, "The first thing my best friend said to me when I told her what happened was, 'Well, I knew you shouldn't have worn that shirt when you went out with Lee. I'm sure he thought you wanted some.' "

Groans fill the room. "Some best friend," can be heard from one woman.

Twice a month these women share thoughts like these. They complain about husbands or boyfriends who can't understand. They praise the ones who do. The counselor running the session asks if anyone has anything to tell Maddie on her first day. One woman who was raped a year earlier doesn't hesitate. She says, "Two things. One: It wasn't your fault. Two: It'll be okay."

ble with relationships after an attack. And often the victim's sex life is affected because sex brings back memories of the attack.

Other victims become **promiscuous** after a rape. They may feel that their partners will take sex forcibly unless they "give it away." Such an attitude can also make a rape victim feel she's gotten back the control she thinks she lost. By deciding to have sex before her partner even asks, a rape victim has basically kept control over her own sex life. She may also openly say yes to sex so that doubts about her consent can't make her blame herself again.

Frequently the victim closes off her mind to the attack. She tries to forget all the details. But one day a smell or a song or some other detail that reminds the victim of the rape can bring the memories rushing back.

Many victims experience what is called **rape trauma syndrome** (RTS). The victim relives her attack over and over, through flashbacks and nightmares. Symptoms of this syndrome include insomnia, loss of appetite, and lack of concentration. RTS victims also spend a lot of time avoiding the things that remind them of the rape.

This reaction is a form of **posttraumatic stress disorder**. It is similar in many ways to the reaction many Vietnam veterans experienced after returning from the war. Like the vets, the victim may have this reaction right after the incident, or years or even decades later.

The best way for a victim to face these traumas is to get

counseling. Rape crisis centers handle victims who have just been raped. But they also deal with victims who don't seek help until years after their attack. Counseling is essential for every victim. It can help a woman realize that her reactions are normal. With the help of counseling, women learn that they can still have meaningful, healthy relationships.

Rallies and conferences help young people become aware of date rape and what they can do to avoid it.

FOR MORE
INFORMATION

The National Organization for Women (NOW)
100 16th Street NW, Suite 700
Washington, D.C. 20036
(202) 331-0066

The National Youth Crisis Hotline
(800) 448-4663

Local rape hot lines or rape crisis centers are listed in the
phone book under "Rape."

GLOSSARY/ INDEX

DEFENDANT—*36*   A person against whom a legal action is brought (the accused in a criminal case or the person being sued in a civil case).

DEGRADE—*8*   To humiliate, shame, or cause someone to lose feelings of self-respect.

DISTRICT ATTORNEY—*35*   The lawyer for the state or city in a criminal case; also called prosecutor.

EVIDENCE COLLECTION KIT—*35*   A medical kit used to take samples of hair, fibers, and fluids from a rape victim. The evidence can be used against the attacker in a criminal case.

GANG RAPE—*29*   A situation in which a group of people force one person to have sex.

HETEROSEXUAL—*18*   One who prefers sex with a member of the opposite sex.

HIV—*35*   The virus that causes AIDS.

HOMOSEXUAL—*18*   One who prefers sex with a member of the same sex.

MARITAL RAPE—*7*   Forced intercourse or sexual acts between a husband and wife.

POSTTRAUMATIC STRESS DISORDER—*40*   The series of emotions felt by the survivor of a serious trauma or unpleasant experience. Symptoms usually include nightmares, anxiety, sleeplessness, and inability to eat.

PROBATION—*35*   The period when a convicted criminal is supervised by the justice system but is not in prison.

PROMISCUOUS—*40*   Having a casual and random attitude about sexual relations; not holding strict morals about sexual behavior.

RAPE—*5*   Forced penetration of the vagina, anus, or mouth with the penis or other object.

RAPE TRAUMA SYNDROME—*40*   Posttraumatic stress disorder as experienced by rape victims. It includes symptoms such as self-blame, reliving the rape experience, problems with sexuality, and the inability to eat and sleep.

REVICTIMIZATION—*18*   The rape of a previous victim of rape or sexual assault, usually because the victim doesn't admit what happened to him or her.

SEMEN—*35*   The sperm-carrying discharge from the penis.

SENTENCE—35   The punishment of a person convicted of a crime. It usually includes time in jail or probation.

SEXUAL ASSAULT—5   Physical, sexual advances against a person who does not consent, with or without actual intercourse.

SEXUALLY TRANSMITTED DISEASE—32   A disease given to others through sexual contact. Examples are AIDS, herpes, syphilis, and gonorrhea.

STRANGER RAPE—7   Forced sexual intercourse or sexual acts between two people who do not know each other.